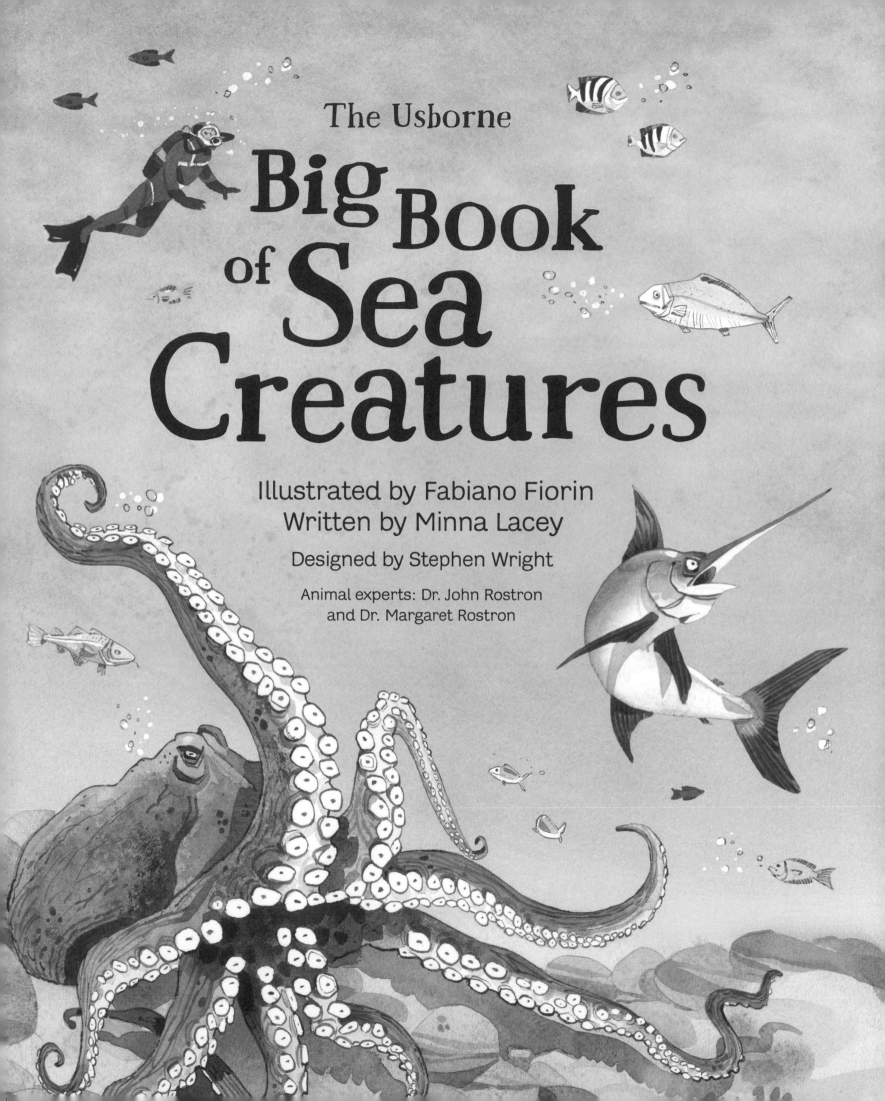

The Usborne
Big Book of Sea Creatures

Illustrated by Fabiano Fiorin
Written by Minna Lacey

Designed by Stephen Wright

Animal experts: Dr. John Rostron
and Dr. Margaret Rostron

Coral reef

A coral reef is home to all sorts of amazing sea creatures. It is made from the skeletons of lots of tiny animals and takes thousands of years to grow.

Remora fish

A **parrotfish** has teeth outside its jaws to help it crunch up coral to eat.

White-tipped reef sharks are named after the white tips on their fins.

A **lionfish** has spiky fins with poisonous tips.

This GIANT **manta ray** sometimes leaps high out of the water. A fully grown ray can reach a massive 7m (23ft) in width.

Emperor angelfish

It uses these mouth flaps to gather up tiny animals and plants to eat.

A **giant barrel sponge** can live for more than 1,000 years. This one is taller than a man.

Sea cucumbers crawl slowly along the reef grabbing food with their sticky tentacles.

Blue whales usually come to the surface to breathe every four minutes. But when diving for food they can stay beneath the water for 30 minutes.

Atlantic walruses feed mostly on shellfish. They can suck the soft flesh out of shells in a few seconds.

Bottlenose dolphins make whistling and clicking noises to send signals to each other.

Killer whales have the largest dorsal fins of any whale or dolphin. Some fins grow 2m (6ft) high – as tall as a man.

A **humpback whale** is a powerful swimmer that often leaps out of the water.

Animals called barnacles grow on its skin.

Mammals

Some of the biggest and most extraordinary animals in the sea are vast mammals that swim and hunt underwater but come to the surface to breathe.

South American sea lions hunt for fish, squid and small penguins close to the shore.
Length: over 2½m (8ft)

Lift the pages to see ocean mammals drawn roughly to scale.

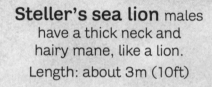

Atlantic walruses use their tusks for fighting and hauling themselves onto the Arctic ice.
Length: up to 3m (10ft)

Steller's sea lion males have a thick neck and hairy mane, like a lion.
Length: about 3m (10ft)

Killer whales are the largest kind of dolphin.
Length: up to 10m (33ft)

Fin whales are the second longest whale after the blue whale.
Length: up to 27m (89ft)

Inside its mouth are hundreds of plates that act as a net for catching tiny shrimp-like creatures called krill.

Blue whales are the biggest creatures that have ever lived. They make a loud rumbling noise that can be heard from far across the ocean.
Length: over 30m (100ft) – as long as four buses parked end to end.

Octopuses, squid & jellyfish

Octopuses, squid and jellyfish have soft bodies and no shell. They have writhing arms or poisonous tentacles to help them catch prey.

A **common Atlantic octopus** has eight arms. It lies waiting in the rocks, then quickly grabs crabs or shrimp to eat.

A **lion's mane jellyfish** is the biggest jellyfish in the world. It floats near the surface and lives for only a year.

Its tentacles are so long they could stretch across the length of a tennis court.

Each arm has powerful suckers to catch and hold onto prey.

This octopus can change its shade to blend in with its background.

Male **southern elephant seals** fight and roar loudly to defend a piece of land. They can live without food for three months while guarding a space.

Leopard seals take their name from the black spots on their fur.

Sea lions often hunt in groups for fish, squid, octopuses and crabs.

Sperm whales are the biggest hunters in the ocean. They often attack giant squid deep below the surface.

Blue whales breathe through two blow holes on top of their head.

Southern elephant seals
get their name from the male's big nose,
which looks a little like an elephant's trunk.
Length: up to 5m (16ft)

Bottlenose dolphins
are highly intelligent and
live in warm waters.
Length: 4m (13ft)

Leopard seals are fierce
hunters that grab fish, small
seals and penguins to eat.
Length: more than 3m (10ft)

Common long-beaked dolphins
swim fast in groups, called pods,
of up to a thousand dolphins.
Length: 2½m (8ft)

Dugongs graze on
sea grass close to the
shore. Unlike seals, they
cannot live on land.
Length: up to 3m (10ft)

West Indian manatees
move slowly near the
surface, grazing on plants.
Length: 4m (13ft)

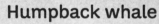

Humpback whale
males sing a magical
song that lasts
for many hours.
Length: up to 16m (52ft)

Sperm whales dive deeper than
any other mammal and can stay
underwater for up to two hours.
Length: up to 18m (60ft)

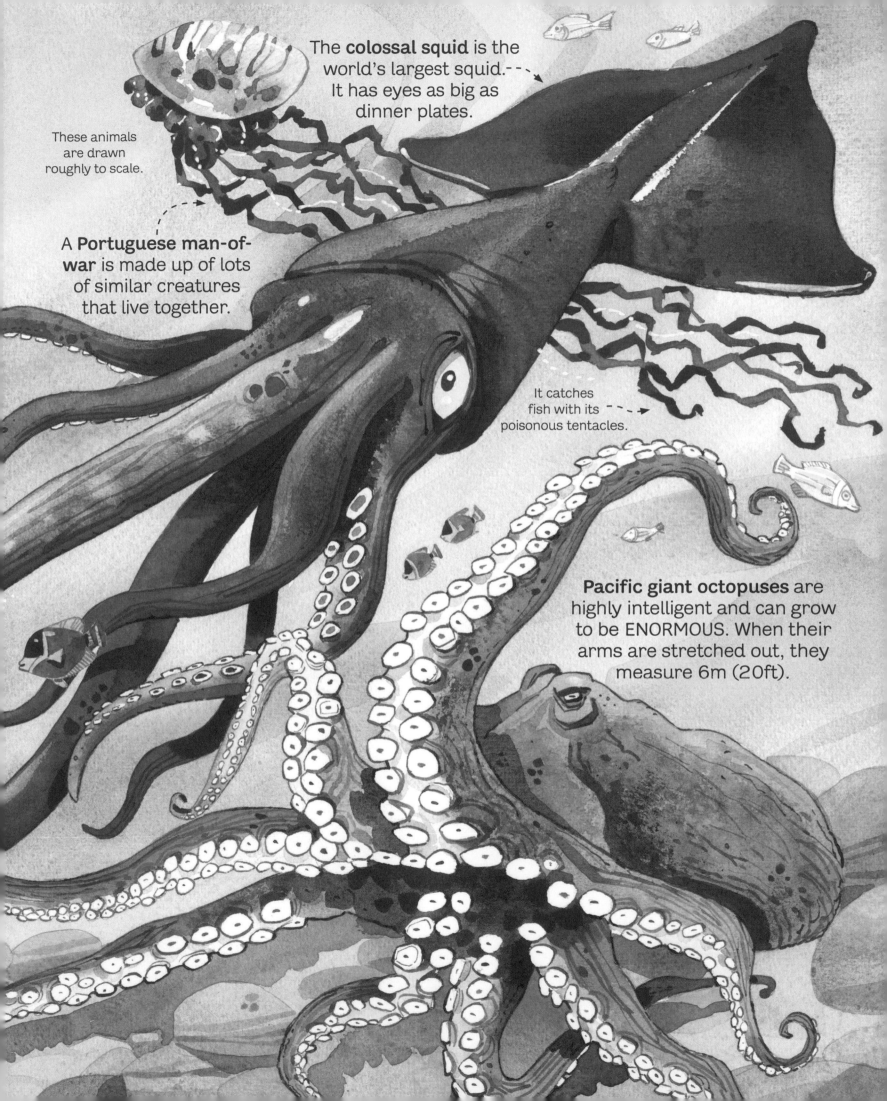

The **colossal squid** is the world's largest squid. It has eyes as big as dinner plates.

These animals are drawn roughly to scale.

A **Portuguese man-of-war** is made up of lots of similar creatures that live together.

It catches fish with its poisonous tentacles.

Pacific giant octopuses are highly intelligent and can grow to be ENORMOUS. When their arms are stretched out, they measure 6m (20ft).

Animals with shells

Many sea creatures have soft bodies with hard shells or bony skeletons on the outside, to give them protection from hungry predators.

All sea turtles have a shell on their backs – except the **leatherback sea turtle**, which has a tough, leathery skin instead.

A **giant clam** has a huge shell with four or five folds in it. It can live for 100 years and stays in the same place all its life.

This is the clam's mouth. It uses it to suck up tiny animals called plankton.

This bluish shade is produced by plants called algae that live on the clam.

The **emperor nautilus** has a striking brown and white shell with many compartments inside. It swims along by sucking in and shooting out jets of water.

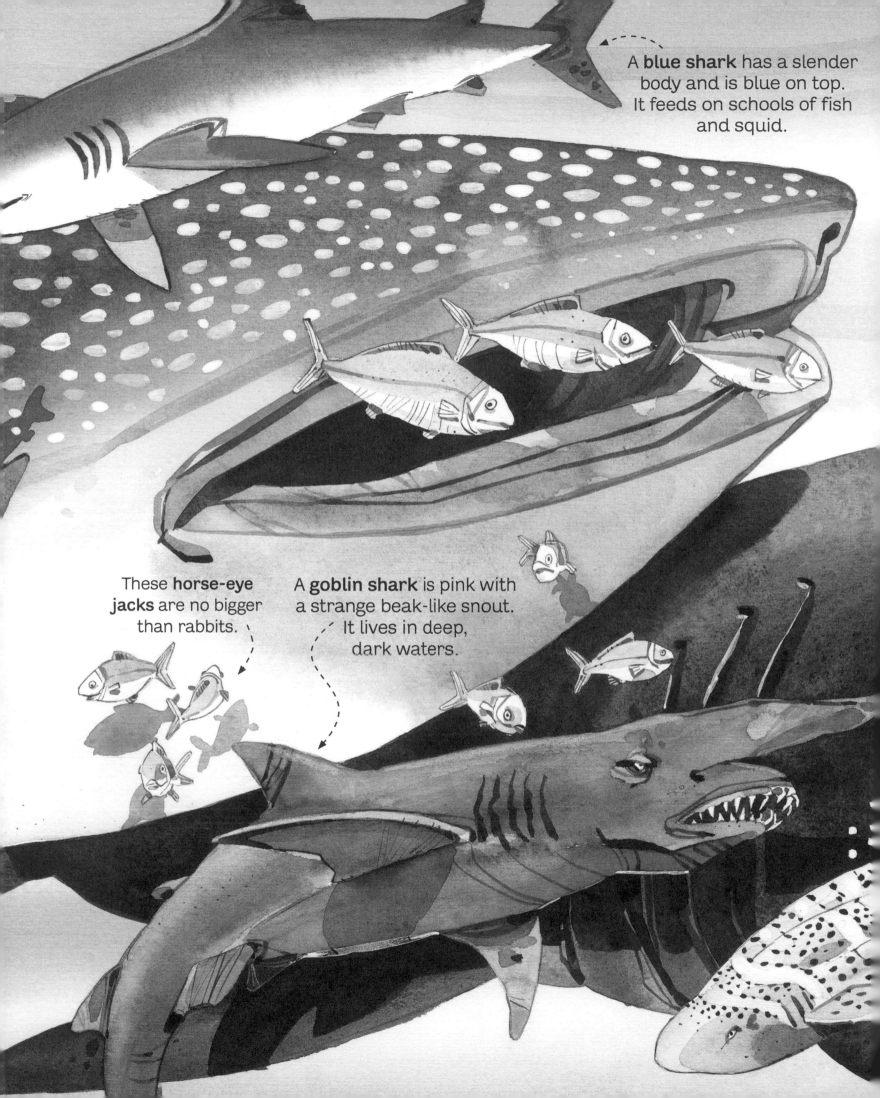

A **blue shark** has a slender body and is blue on top. It feeds on schools of fish and squid.

These **horse-eye jacks** are no bigger than rabbits.

A **goblin shark** is pink with a strange beak-like snout. It lives in deep, dark waters.

Large front flippers help it move swiftly through the water. The turtle grows to a massive 3m (10ft) in length – that's as long as a tiger.

Its eyes move in different directions.

Atlantic lobsters are one of the largest lobsters. In real life, they're four times as long as this.

Its bigger claw is used for crushing crabs and fish to eat.

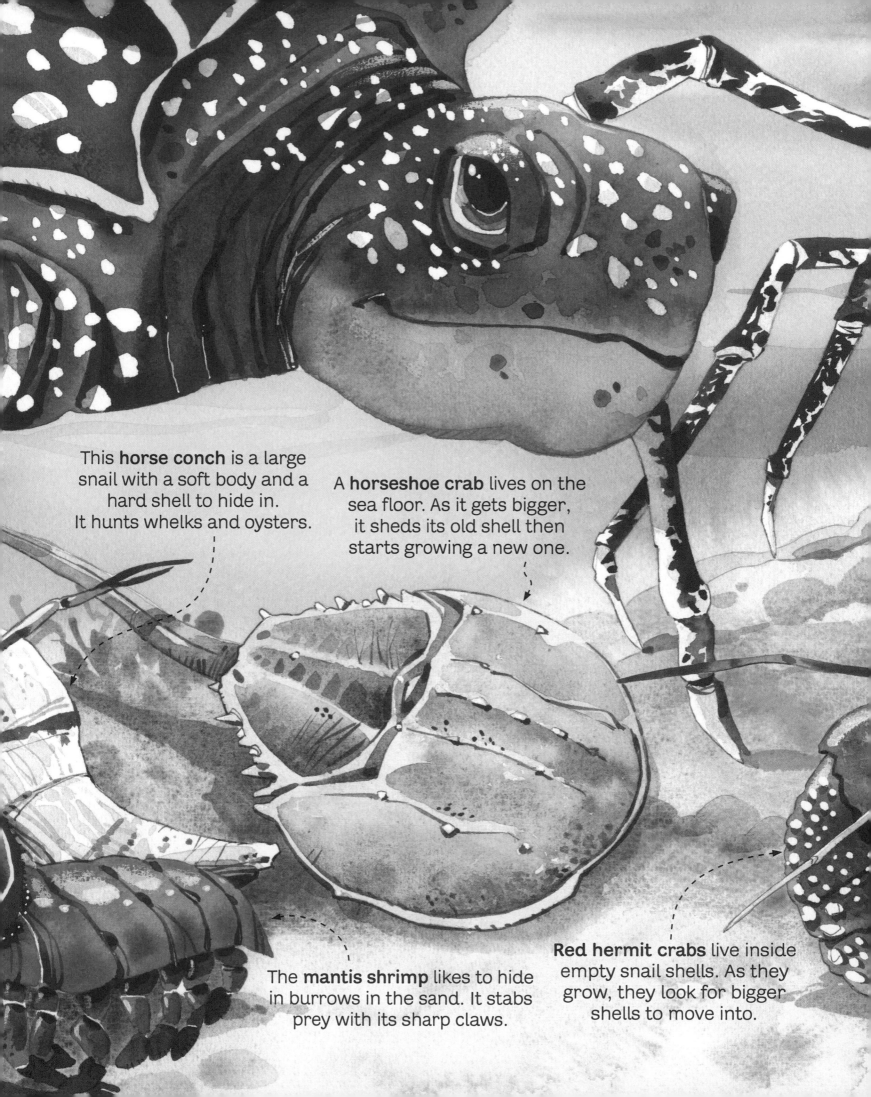

This **horse conch** is a large snail with a soft body and a hard shell to hide in. It hunts whelks and oysters.

A **horseshoe crab** lives on the sea floor. As it gets bigger, it sheds its old shell then starts growing a new one.

The **mantis shrimp** likes to hide in burrows in the sand. It stabs prey with its sharp claws.

Red hermit crabs live inside empty snail shells. As they grow, they look for bigger shells to move into.

A **whale shark** is the biggest kind of fish. It has no teeth and grows to a massive 14m (46ft) – that's longer than a bus.

Sharks breathe through these gill slits.

A fully grown **epaulette shark** has a large black spot on its shoulder.

Sharks

A shark is a big fish with a soft skeleton made of cartilage, not bone. Many sharks are fierce hunters, but the biggest are toothless and feed on tiny shrimp.

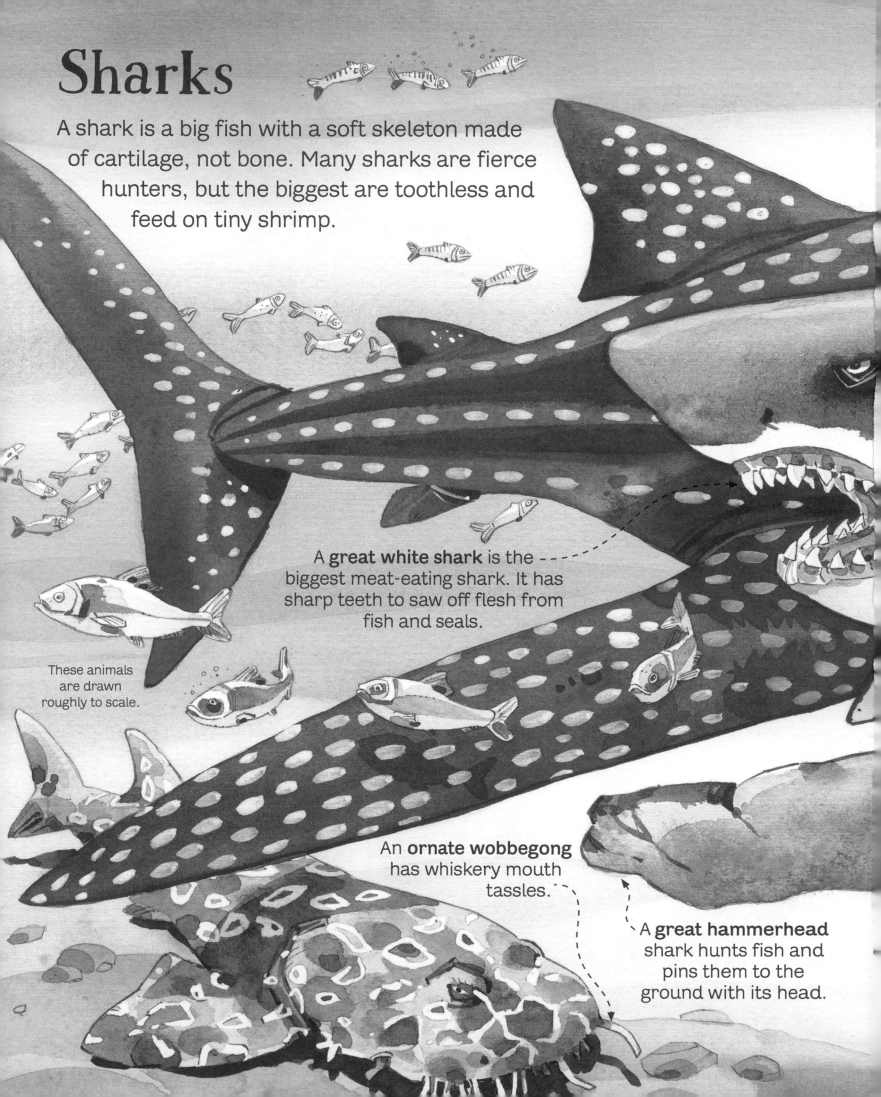

A **great white shark** is the biggest meat-eating shark. It has sharp teeth to saw off flesh from fish and seals.

These animals are drawn roughly to scale.

An **ornate wobbegong** has whiskery mouth tassles.

A **great hammerhead** shark hunts fish and pins them to the ground with its head.

This **Japanese spider crab** has extremely long legs that stretch 4m (13ft) from claw to claw. It feeds on shellfish and can live for 100 years.

Even its body is the size of a basketball.

This **giant triton** shell is twice as big as a motorcycle helmet.

Big fish

All fish breathe through gills at the sides of their heads. Most fish have a skeleton made of bone – except sharks and rays.

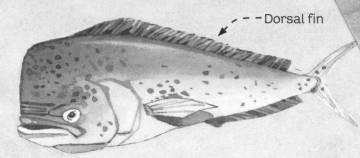

- - Dorsal fin

Mahi mahi have huge foreheads and long dorsal fins along their backs.
Length: up to 2m (6½ft)

Bluefin tuna are one of the fastest and biggest bony fish.
Length: up to 3m (10ft)

The gills are under here.

Humphead wrasse are some of the largest fish that live on coral reefs. They have a big bulge on their heads.
Length: up to 2m (6½ft)

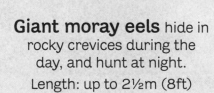

Giant moray eels hide in rocky crevices during the day, and hunt at night.
Length: up to 2½m (8ft)

- - This sharp sword-shaped bill is used to slash at prey.

Lift the pages to see big fish drawn roughly to scale.

Swordfish are fast and acrobatic. They perform magnificent leaps out of the water.
Length: up to 4½m (15ft)

Some are taller - from fin to fin than they are long.

Ocean sunfish are the largest kind of bony fish. They often swim slowly near the surface.
Length: up to 3½m (12ft)

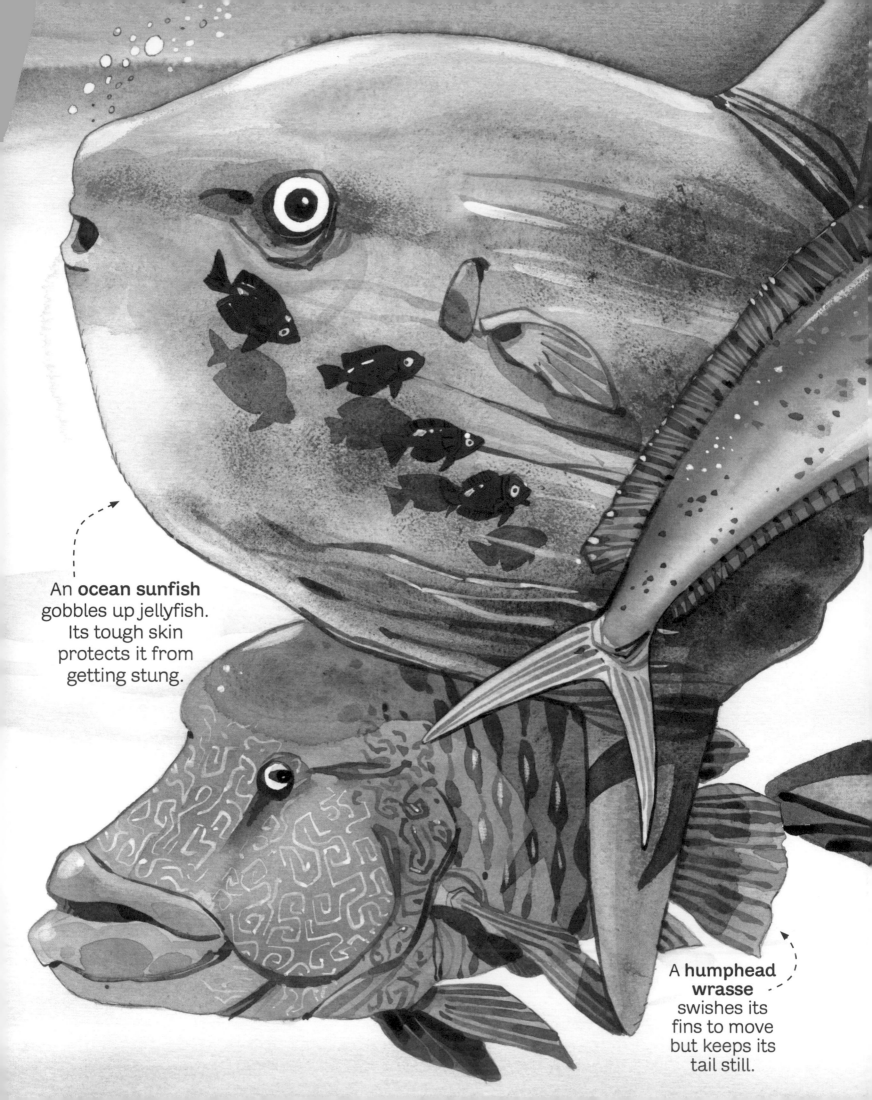

An **ocean sunfish** gobbles up jellyfish. Its tough skin protects it from getting stung.

A **humphead wrasse** swishes its fins to move but keeps its tail still.

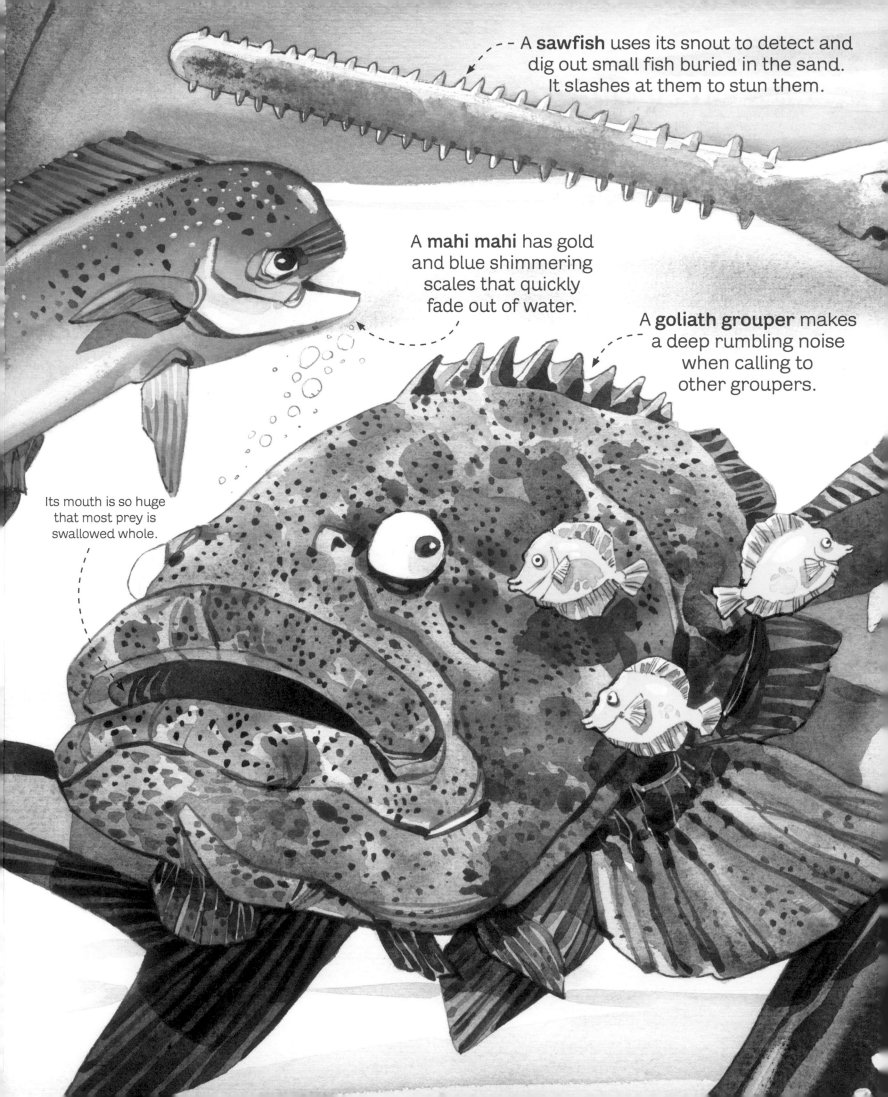

A **sawfish** uses its snout to detect and dig out small fish buried in the sand. It slashes at them to stun them.

A **mahi mahi** has gold and blue shimmering scales that quickly fade out of water.

A **goliath grouper** makes a deep rumbling noise when calling to other groupers.

Its mouth is so huge that most prey is swallowed whole.

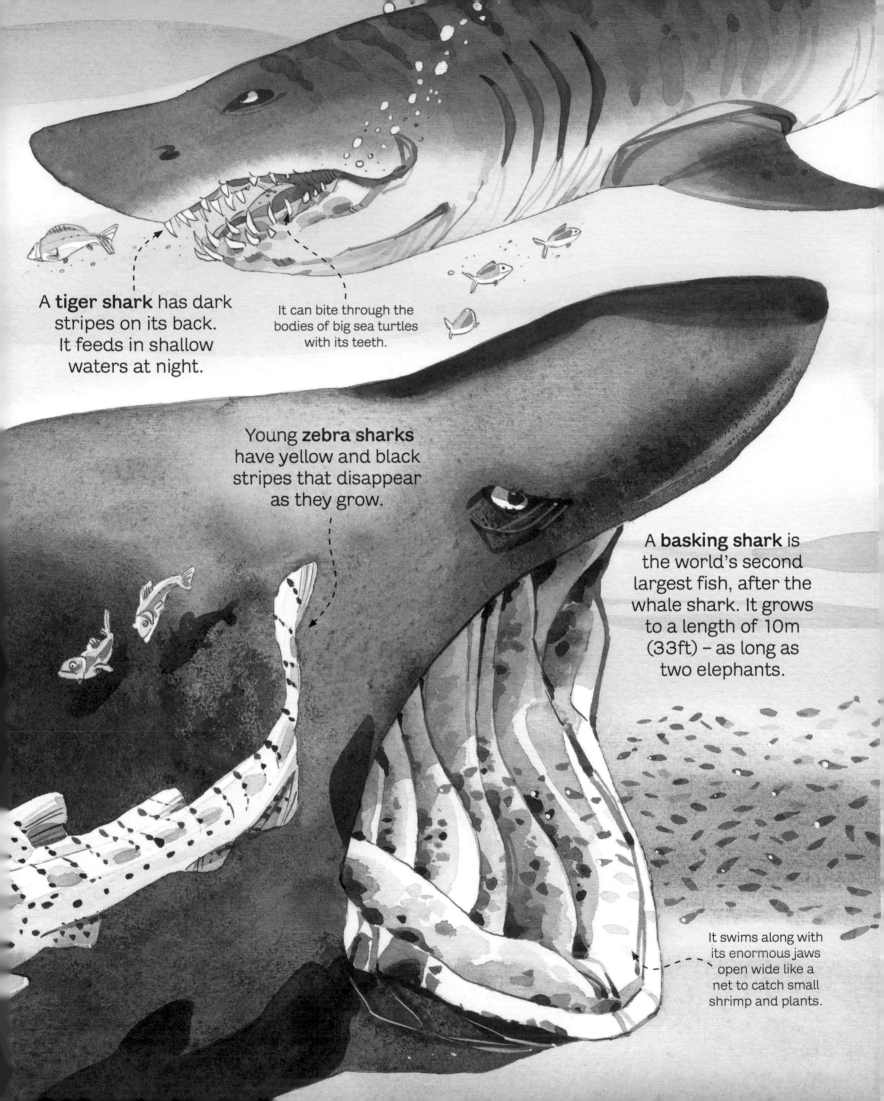

A **tiger shark** has dark
stripes on its back.
It feeds in shallow
waters at night.

It can bite through the
bodies of big sea turtles
with its teeth.

Young **zebra sharks**
have yellow and black
stripes that disappear
as they grow.

A **basking shark** is
the world's second
largest fish, after the
whale shark. It grows
to a length of 10m
(33ft) – as long as
two elephants.

It swims along with
its enormous jaws
open wide like a
net to catch small
shrimp and plants.

Biggest, fastest, longest...

The **southern elephant seal** is the BIGGEST of all seals, sea lions or walruses.

The **whale shark** is the BIGGEST FISH in the ocean. It gulps down mouthfuls of water in its enormous mouth to catch very tiny animals and plants to eat.

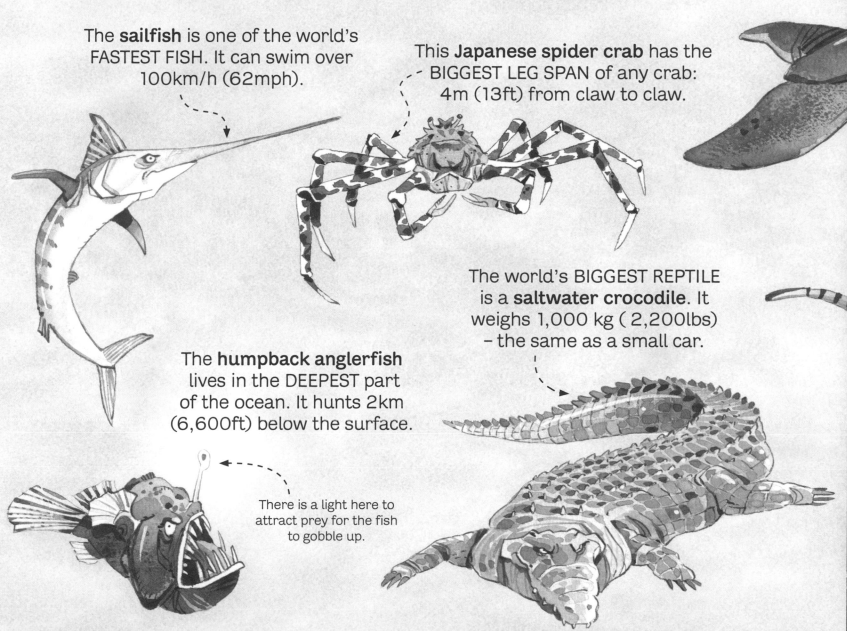

The **sailfish** is one of the world's FASTEST FISH. It can swim over 100km/h (62mph).

This **Japanese spider crab** has the BIGGEST LEG SPAN of any crab: 4m (13ft) from claw to claw.

The world's BIGGEST REPTILE is a **saltwater crocodile**. It weighs 1,000 kg (2,200lbs) – the same as a small car.

The **humpback anglerfish** lives in the DEEPEST part of the ocean. It hunts 2km (6,600ft) below the surface.

There is a light here to attract prey for the fish to gobble up.

Giant moray eels have sharp teeth for tearing the flesh of small fish, crabs or octopuses.

Conger eels are often found in shipwrecks and rocky pools. They feed on crabs, shrimp and octopuses.

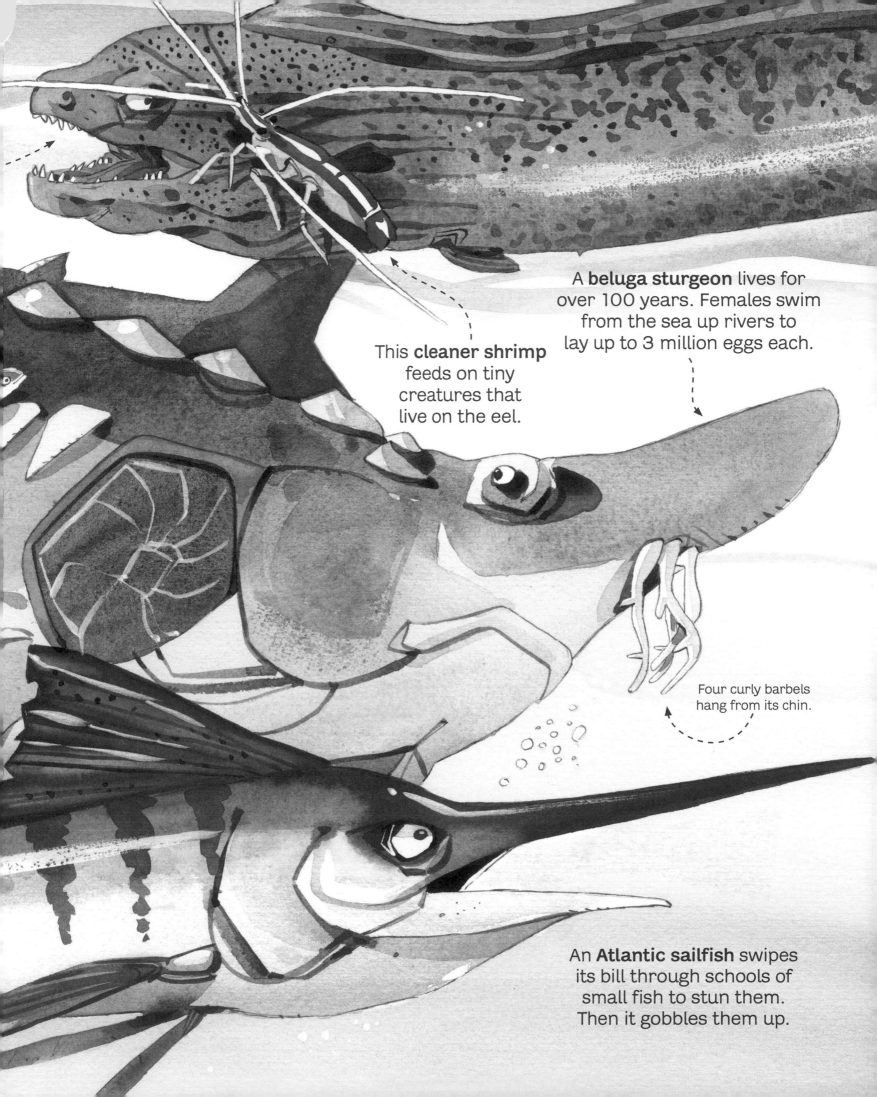

This **cleaner shrimp** feeds on tiny creatures that live on the eel.

A **beluga sturgeon** lives for over 100 years. Females swim from the sea up rivers to lay up to 3 million eggs each.

Four curly barbels hang from its chin.

An **Atlantic sailfish** swipes its bill through schools of small fish to stun them. Then it gobbles them up.

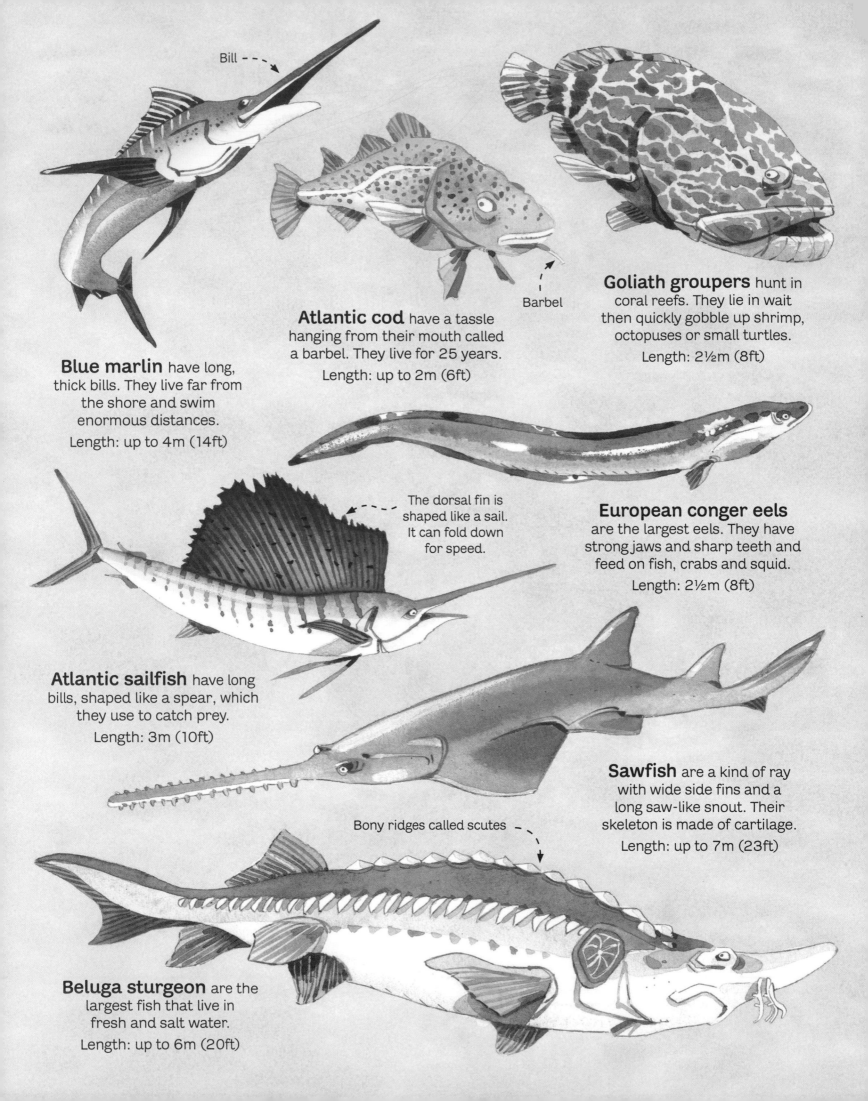

Bill - - - >

Goliath groupers hunt in coral reefs. They lie in wait then quickly gobble up shrimp, octopuses or small turtles.

Length: 2½m (8ft)

Atlantic cod have a tassle hanging from their mouth called a barbel. They live for 25 years.

Length: up to 2m (6ft)

Barbel

Blue marlin have long, thick bills. They live far from the shore and swim enormous distances.

Length: up to 4m (14ft)

The dorsal fin is shaped like a sail. It can fold down for speed.

European conger eels are the largest eels. They have strong jaws and sharp teeth and feed on fish, crabs and squid.

Length: 2½m (8ft)

Atlantic sailfish have long bills, shaped like a spear, which they use to catch prey.

Length: 3m (10ft)

Sawfish are a kind of ray with wide side fins and a long saw-like snout. Their skeleton is made of cartilage.

Length: up to 7m (23ft)

Bony ridges called scutes - - >

Beluga sturgeon are the largest fish that live in fresh and salt water.

Length: up to 6m (20ft)

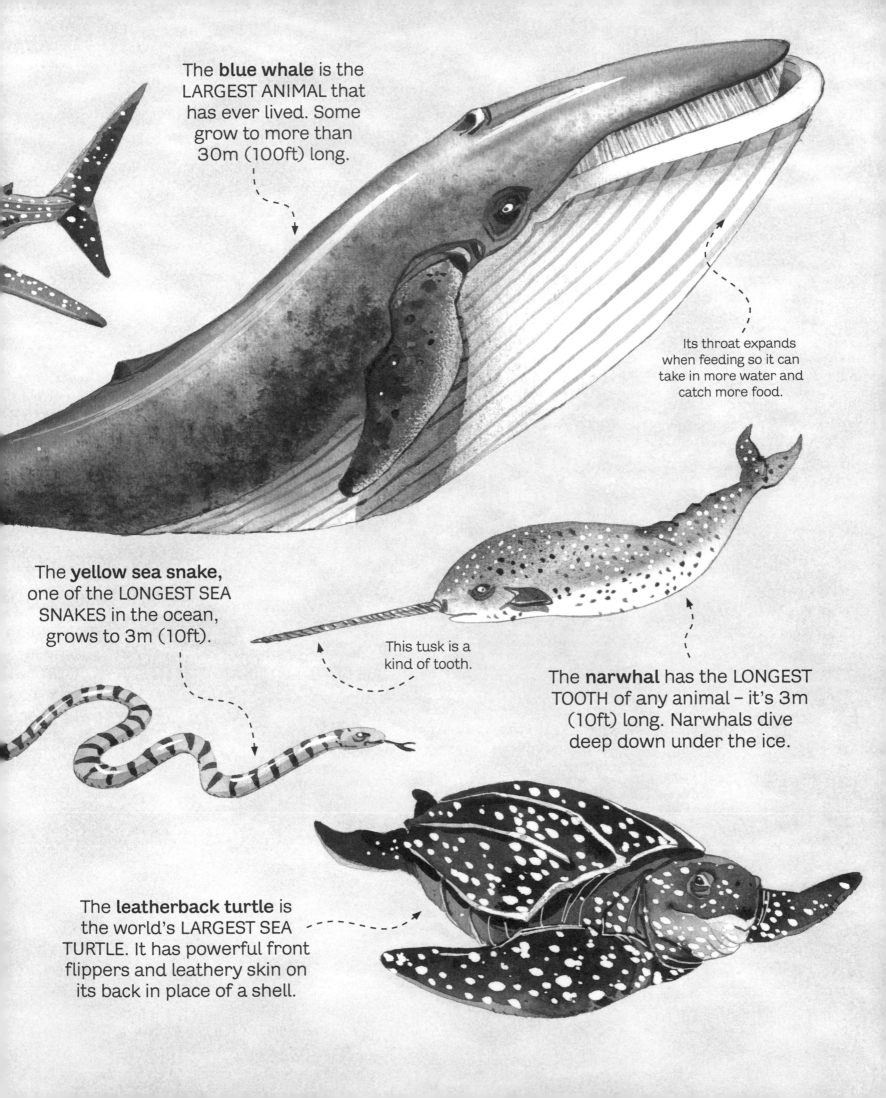

The **blue whale** is the LARGEST ANIMAL that has ever lived. Some grow to more than 30m (100ft) long.

Its throat expands when feeding so it can take in more water and catch more food.

The **yellow sea snake**, one of the LONGEST SEA SNAKES in the ocean, grows to 3m (10ft).

This tusk is a kind of tooth.

The **narwhal** has the LONGEST TOOTH of any animal – it's 3m (10ft) long. Narwhals dive deep down under the ice.

The **leatherback turtle** is the world's LARGEST SEA TURTLE. It has powerful front flippers and leathery skin on its back in place of a shell.

Series editor: Jane Chisholm
Additional design: Nelupa Hussain and Vickie Robinson
Image manipulation: Nick Wakeford and John Russell

This edition first published in 2016 by Usborne Publishing Ltd., Usborne House, 83-85 Saffron Hill, London EC1N 8RT,
England. www.usborne.com Copyright © 2016, 2011 Usborne Publishing Ltd.